MW01015730

Grade Boosters

BOOSTING YOUR WAY TO SUCCESS IN SCHOOL

Second Grade Reading

By Faybeth Harter

Illustrated by Eve Guianan

LOWELL HOUSE JUVENILE

LOS ANGELES

CONTEMPORY BOOKS

CHICAGO

To my children—Ken, Dave, Leanne, and Tom—and my grandchildren—
Kayla, T.C., Johnny, Christina, and ?

—F.H.

Reviewed and endorsed by Susan C. Hay, M.A.,
veteran education and elementary reading and curriculum specialist

About the Author
Faybeth Harter has taught reading to all age groups for more than twenty years. With a Masters of Education in reading, her expertise encompasses all areas of reading education, including remedial, developmental, and speed. Harter is currently teaching adult education for the Garden Grove Unified School District in California. She also instructs teacher development courses and serves on the Western Association of Schools and Colleges accreditation committees for the State of California.

Requests for such permissions should be addressed to:
Lowell House Juvenile
2020 Avenue of the Stars, Suite 300
Los Angeles, CA 90067

Publisher: Jack Artenstein
Associate Publisher, Juvenile Division: Elizabeth D. Amos
Director of Publishing Services: Rena Copperman
Managing Editor, Juvenile Division: Lindsey Hay
Editor in Chief, Juvenile Nonfiction: Amy Downing
Project Editor: Jessica Oifer

Lowell House books can be purchased at special discounts when ordered in bulk for premiums and special sales. Contact Department JH at the above address.

Manufactured in the United States of America

ISBN: 1-56565-512-5

10 9 8 7 6 5 4 3 2 1

BOOSTING SUCCESS IN READING

When children can read, they can learn just about anything they desire. A world of possibilities awaits them. But when they can't read, they become easily frustrated and embarrassed. Learning—an activity that once came naturally to them—is no longer a pleasure. **GRADE BOOSTERS: Second Grade Reading** lets your child experience learning in a stimulating, educational way.

While there is no one sure way to learn to read, nor any foolproof formula to teach reading, the *process* of learning to read always begins with the basics: recognition of the consonants and their associated sounds, and learning the various phonetic usages of the vowels. The auditory recognition of the consonants and vowels is crucial to sounding out unrecognized words as your child is beginning to read.

Once your child can recognize words, their meanings can be understood. As important as each word can be, without comprehension—a critical thinking skill—all reading is meaningless. Integrating word recognition with concepts and ideas leads to the development of that comprehension.

How to Use This Book

GRADE BOOSTERS: Second Grade Reading offers your child opportunities to review the consonants and vowels—both long and short. The book is divided into four major sections: the review, word recognition and construction, reasoning skills, and comprehension skills.

Your child has an opportunity to make visual and auditory connections as he or she explores the various forms and constructions of words. This involves completing fun activities using synonyms, antonyms, and homonyms. Your child will also learn and work with compounds, rhyming words, plurals, contractions, and syllables.

Reasoning skills are taught and reinforced through classification, categorizing, and comparison exercises. Your child also will practice sequencing and following directions. Activities on cause and effect as well as fact versus opinion further tap into your child's reasoning skills.

The comprehension exercises integrate word recognition with under-standing overall concepts and ideas. Children gain practice and reinforcement by choosing the main idea of short passages and then drawing conclusions that utilize critical thinking skills.

Ending each section is a Review Test, which checks your child's progress on mastering the various reading skills. Achievement awards help develop your child's sense of accomplishment and academic success.

Note to Parents

Two important features also appear throughout the book. TOGETHER TIME, designed especially for interactive learning, offers activities for you and your child to do together. The GRADE BOOSTER! feature specifically promotes critical and creative thinking skills. These are precisely the skills that will become vital to your child's future academic success—and success in life.

Time Spent Together

The time you spend with your child as he or she learns is invaluable. Therefore, the more positive and constructive environment you can create, the better. In working together, allow your child the freedom to go at his or her own pace. If your child would like to talk about the pictures, all the better. Allow your child to freely share and express opinions. Ask questions about what your child sees. Be creative! Encourage your child to predict actions or events, or even make up a story about what he or she sees on the page.

Remember to consider your child's ability. Because the activities range from easy to more difficult, you may need to work with your child on many of the pages. Read the directions and explain them. Go over the examples that are given. While creativity should be encouraged and praised, help your child look for the best answer.

Work together only as long as he or she remains interested. If necessary, practice a single section or word at a time. Before going on to a new word, always review work just completed. That will ensure better recall. The exercises should be done consecutively, as the activities on each page build on the skills presented on the pages that precede it. Remember that eagerness, willingness, and success are much more important in the long run than exactness or perfection. Remember, too, that your child's level of participation will vary at different times. Sometimes a response may be brief and simplistic; at other times, a response may be elaborate and creative. Allow room for both. Much more learning will take place in a secure, accepting environment.

Positive experiences promote positive attitudes, including a desire to learn and a curiosity about the world. You can be an instrumental tool in helping your child develop a positive attitude toward learning. Your "one-on-one" contact cannot be duplicated at school. Therefore, you have a choice opportunity to share with your child as he or she learns about the world around us.

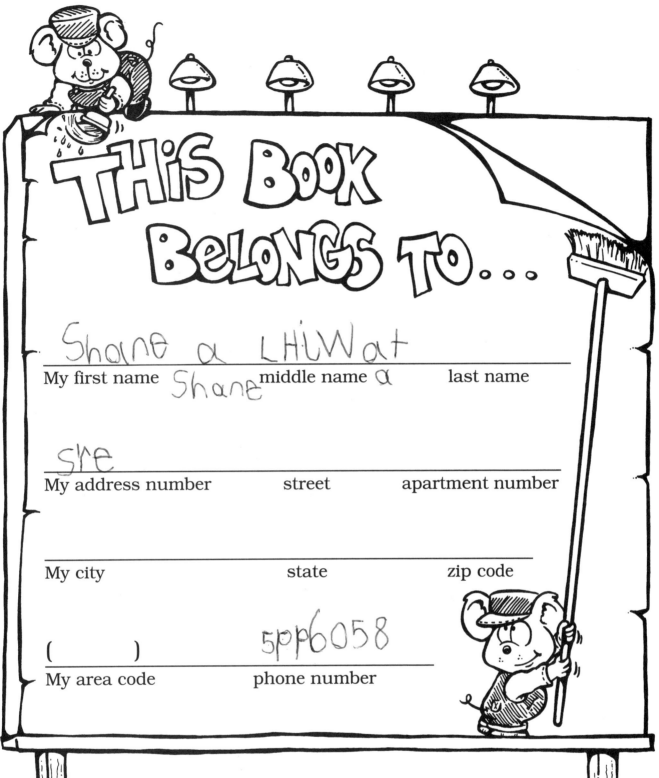

THiS BOOK BELONGS TO...

Shane a LHLWat *(handwritten)*

My first name   Shane *(handwritten)* middle name   a *(handwritten)*   last name

sre *(handwritten)*

My address number   street   apartment number

_____

My city   state   zip code

(   )   5pp6058 *(handwritten)*

My area code   phone number

I know my letters and my sounds. Now I am going to practice using words and reading!

CONSONANT CONNECTION

Look at each picture below. Then write the **consonant** that it starts with on the blank line. The first one is done for you.

B   S   W   K   m

C   B c   Z   P   q

L   t   J D   N   W

f V   X   m R   7 f   H

B C D F G H J K L M N P Q R S T V W X Y Z
b c d f g h j k l m n p q r s t v w x y z

2

GRADE BOOSTER!

*Which two **consonants** are not pictured above? _____ Can you think of words that begin with each of those **consonants**? On a separate piece of paper, write each word and then use it in a sentence.*

Skills: review of consonant recognition, discrimination, creativity

PIES AND CAKES

Do you remember the **long vowel rule**? Well, here it is:

The **long vowel** says its name! When a word has **two** vowels together, the first vowel is **long** and the second vowel is **silent**.

Match the words in the Word Box to their **long vowel** sounds by writing each word under its correct sound.

WORD BOX

rain	feet	fire	kite	tail	rake
bee	slide	pea	seal	baby	child

long ā as in cake

long ē as in tree

long ī as in pie

_____   _____   _____

_____   _____   _____

_____   _____   _____

_____   _____   _____

A SUIT AND A BOAT

Match the words in the Word Box to their **long vowel** sounds by writing each word under its correct sound.

WORD BOX

soap

music

toe

bone

fruit

note

cute

juice

long ō as in boat

_____

_____

_____

_____

long ū as in suit

_____

_____

_____

_____

Did you know that the consonant **Y** makes two different vowel sounds when it appears at the end of a word? It makes the **long ī** sound or the **long ē** sound. Draw a line from each word to the vowel sound it makes.

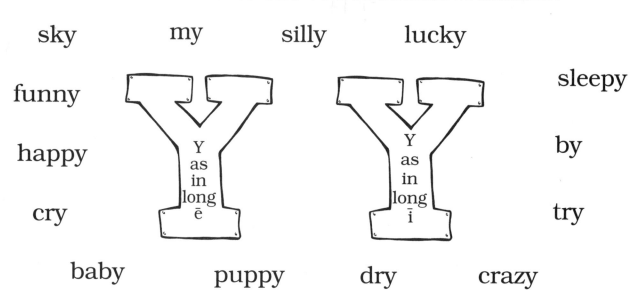

sky   my   silly   lucky

funny   sleepy

happy   Y as in long ē   Y as in long ī   by

cry   try

baby   puppy   dry   crazy

Skills: identifying and associating long vowel sounds, auditory discrimination, deduction

APPLES FOR INSECTS

Now it's time to review the **short vowel** sounds. Match the words in the Word Box to their **short vowel** sounds by writing each word under its correct sound. But be careful! There are some long vowel words hiding in the Word Box!

WORD BOX

pin	cat	tent	swim
nest	eel	mitten	man
bed	pan	kite	airplane

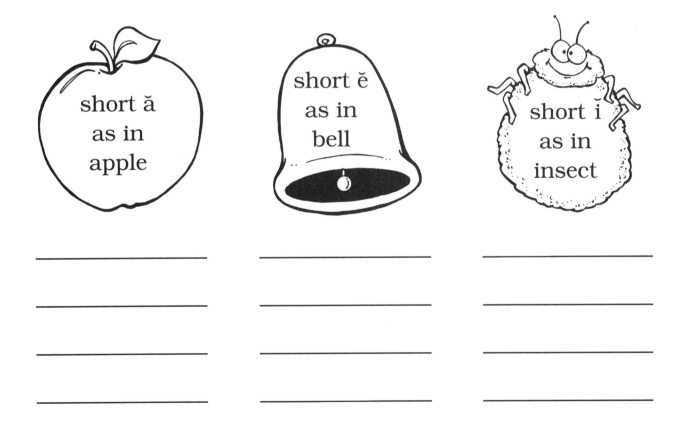

short ă
as in
apple

short ĕ
as in
bell

short i
as in
insect

_____

_____

_____

_____

_____

_____

_____

_____

_____

_____

_____

_____

A ROCKIN' FROG

Match the words in the Word Box to their **short vowel** sounds by writing each word under its correct sound. But be careful! There are some long vowel words hiding in the Word Box!

WORD BOX

sun

box

doll

boot

skunk

nut

toe

octopus

short ŏ
as in frog

short ŭ
as in duck

———————————   ———————————

———————————   ———————————

———————————   ———————————

———————————   ———————————

GRADE BOOSTER!

On a separate piece of paper, write a story about a frog and a duck who live in a pond. Tell about all the wonderful adventures they have together. Use at least two **short ŏ** *words and two* **short ŭ** *words in your story.*

Skills: identifying and associating short vowel sounds, auditory discrimination, deduction, creativity

TEST: Long and Short Vowels

Match each word in the Word Box to its correct picture by writing the word below its picture. Then write the **long** or **short vowel** sound that each word makes on the line provided. Some words may have more than one vowel sound. Then use crayons to color the long vowel words red and the short vowel words blue.

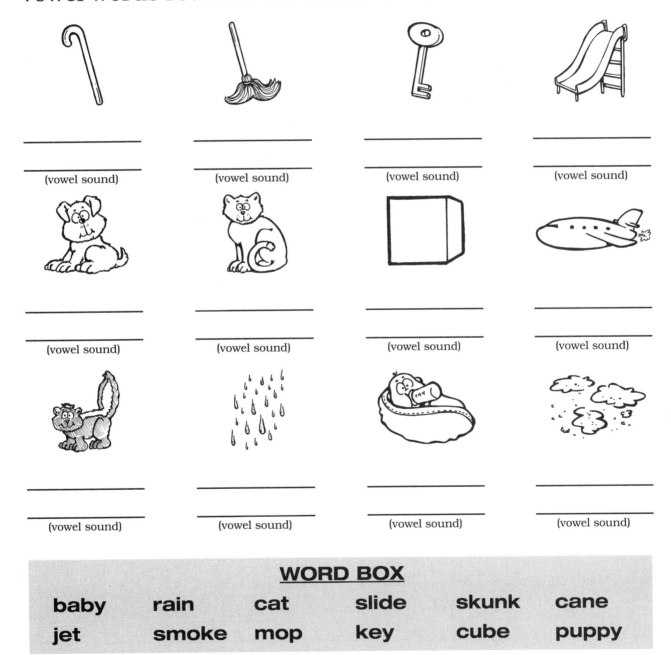

_____

(vowel sound)

_____

(vowel sound)

_____

(vowel sound)

_____

(vowel sound)

_____

(vowel sound)

_____

(vowel sound)

_____

(vowel sound)

_____

(vowel sound)

_____

(vowel sound)

_____

(vowel sound)

_____

(vowel sound)

_____

(vowel sound)

WORD BOX

baby	rain	cat	slide	skunk	cane
jet	smoke	mop	key	cube	puppy

Skills: demonstrating mastery of long and short vowel sounds through testing

11

THE FROG ARTIST

The **R blend** is a consonant combined with the letter **R** to make a special sound.

Frederick likes to **dr**aw with **cr**ayons. Use your favorite color **cr**ayon to **dr**aw a line **fr**om each **R blend** to the picture that it des**cr**ibes.

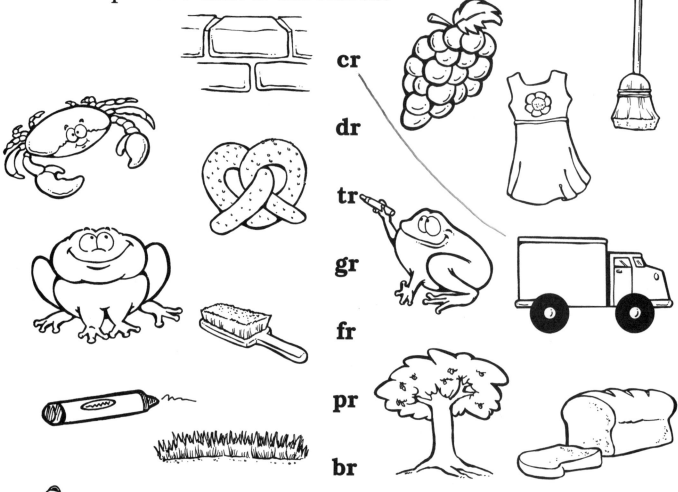

cr

dr

tr

gr

fr

pr

br

GRADE BOOSTER!

*Which **R blend** has the most pictures above?* _____
*Which **R blend** has the least pictures above?* _____

Skills: identifying and associating R consonant blends, auditory and visual discrimination

THE CLOUD-RIDING CLOWN

The **L blend** is a consonant combined with the letter **L** to make a special sound.

sl	cl	bl	fl	pl	gl

Read the sentence below. Circle all the words that begin with an **L blend**.

Clarice the Clown needs glasses to see clearly through the clouds.

Now help Clarice write the **L blend** words below in alphabetical (ABC) order on the blank lines.

blocks   glasses   plane   slide   sleep

flower   flag   blanket   clock

_____   _____   _____

_____   _____   _____

GRADE BOOSTER!

*Below, write another word that begins with each of the **L blends** in the box above.*

_____   _____

_____   _____

_____   _____

SPLISH-SPLASHIN' SHAWN

The **S blend** is a consonant combined with the letter **S** to make a special sound.

Shawn **sp**lashes into the pool of **S blends**. Help him connect each picture to its beginning **S blend** sound by drawing a line between them.

sp

st

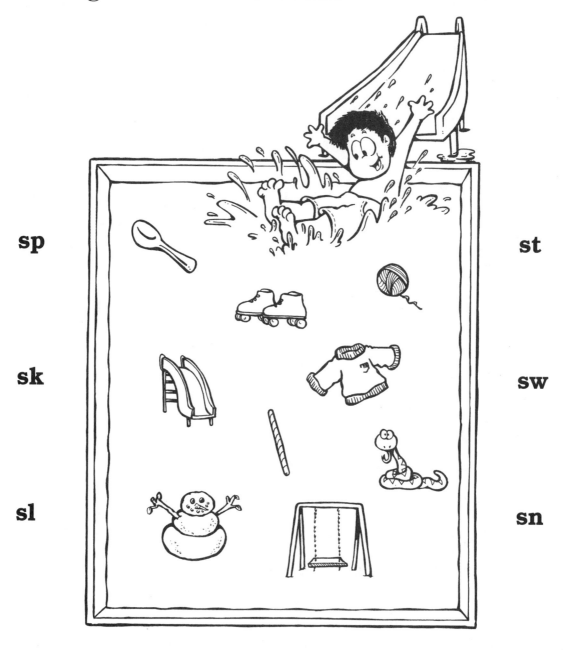

sk

sw

sl

sn

Skills: identifying and associating S consonant blends, auditory and visual discrimination

CHUCKY'S SHOE

A **digraph** is a combination of two different letters that together make a single sound.

Read the following sentence and then circle all the words that contain digraphs of the letter **H**.

Chucky the Chipmunk chuckled and shrieked when he got his shoe caught in the wheel.

Now draw a line connecting each word with the digraph it contains.

wh   **th**   **ch**   **sh**

throat

shoe

shell

whiskers

cherry

cheese

thumb

GRADE BOOSTER!

Think of four more words that contain **digraphs** *of the letter* **H**. *Write them here.*

_____ _____ _____ _____

Skills: identifying and associating digraphs, auditory and visual discrimination

TEST: Consonant Blends
and Digraphs

Circle each consonant blend or digraph that goes with each picture.

dr pr br

sl sh sk

gl pl bl

tr br dr

sm sn sw

cl pl sl

pl cl ck

gr pr tr

sp sc sn

sw sh sc

fl sl gl

pl cl fl

tr br gr

sc sm sn

sh sc sk

sh wh th

ch sh wh

wh ch th

Skills: demonstrating mastery of consonant blends and digraphs through testing

Congratulations!

_____

(my name)

is ready to blast off into the wonderful world of Reading!

(This rocket ship needs a captain!
Draw your picture in the captain's seat.)

THE GREAT SYNONYM MATCH

Words that mean the same or close to the same thing are called **synonyms**. Draw a line from each word on the left side of each book to its **synonym** on the right side. The first word is done for you.

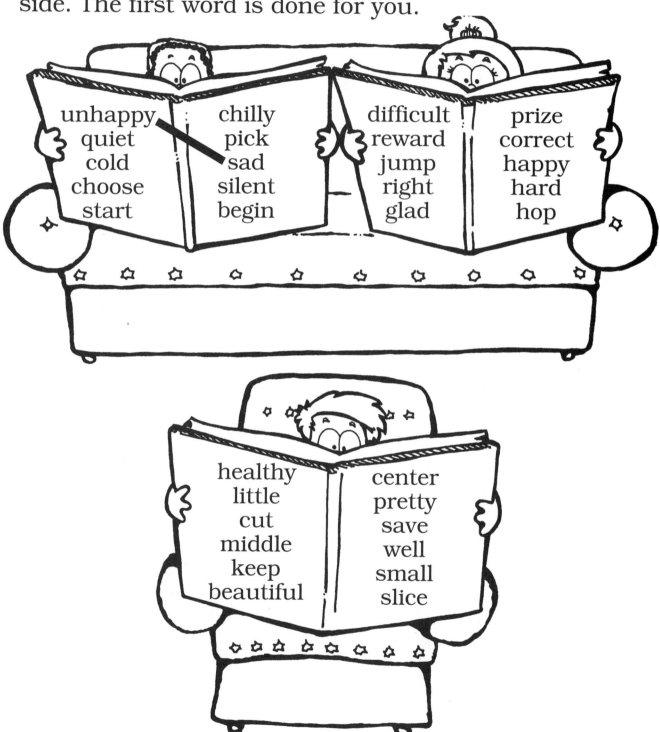

unhappy	chilly	difficult	prize
quiet	pick	reward	correct
cold	sad	jump	happy
choose	silent	right	hard
start	begin	glad	hop

healthy	center
little	pretty
cut	save
middle	well
keep	small
beautiful	slice

Skills: introducing and reinforcing synonyms, reasoning, deduction

SYNONYM SQUARES

Circle the **synonym** on each square that has the same meaning or close to the same meaning as the word in **bold** print. The first one is done for you.

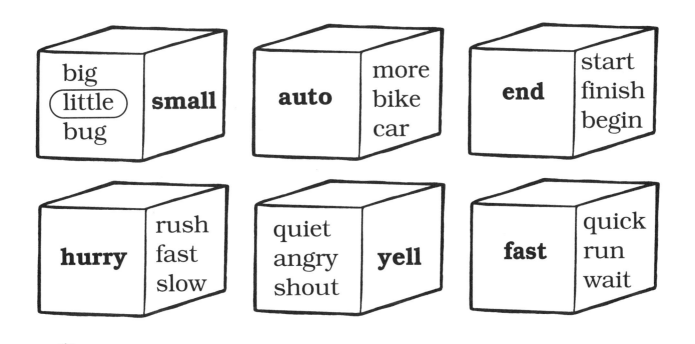

TOGETHER TIME: Ask an adult to help you think of a **synonym** for each of the following words. Write the **synonym** on the line provided. When you're done, grab another piece of paper and use each **synonym** in a sentence.

exam _____   scared _____

large _____   friend _____

maybe _____   fall _____

choose _____   high _____

TEETER-TOTTER OPPOSITES

Words that mean the opposite of each other are called **antonyms**. You probably already know lots of **antonyms**. Use the words in the Word Box to help you find the opposite of the words on the teeter-totters. Then write each **antonym** on the teeter-totter next to its opposite. A few have been done for you.

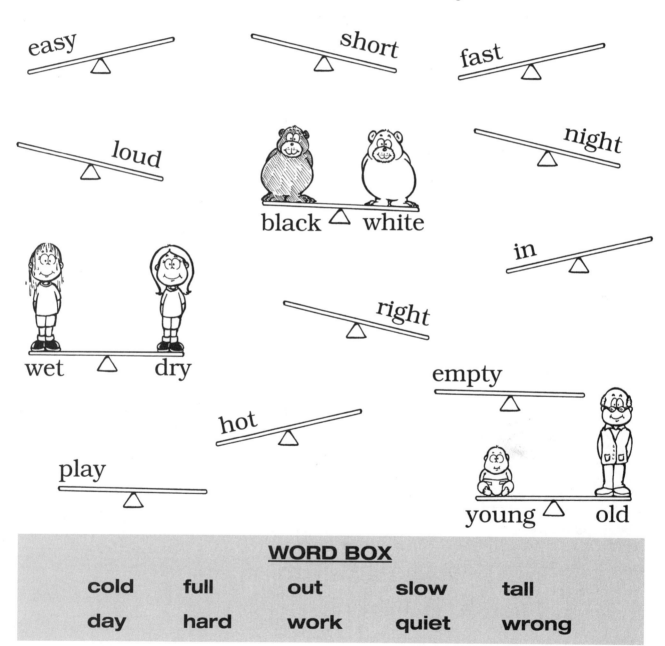

WORD BOX				
cold	full	out	slow	tall
day	hard	work	quiet	wrong

Skills: introducing and reinforcing antonyms, reasoning, deduction

ANDY AND ALLIE

Andy and Allie always do the opposite of each other. When Andy feels cold, Allie is hot. Complete the sentences below so that Andy and Allie always act just like **antonyms**—the opposite of each other.

1. When Andy opens the window,

   Allie _____ it.

2. Allie's room is very _____, but Andy's room

   is dirty.

3. Andy walks near the water, but

   Allie stays _____ from it.

4. Allie turns the light off, but Andy turns it

   _____.

5. Allie has a big dog, but Andy

   has a _____ one.

A GARDEN OF WORDS

Let's review our **synonyms** (same) and **antonyms** (opposite). Use crayons to color the flowers with **synonyms** yellow and the flowers with **antonyms** red.

GRADE BOOSTER!

*How many pairs of **synonyms** did you find? _____*
*How many pairs of **antonyms** did you find? _____*
Are there any flowers that you did not color yellow or red? _____ How many? _____

Skills: discrimination between antonyms and synonyms, deduction

HOMONYM HUNT

Homonyms are words that sound alike but are spelled differently and have different meanings. Match the words in the Word Box to their **homonyms** by writing them under their **homonyms** in the balls. The first one is done for you.

WORD BOX							
blue	male	road	tail	heel	meet	sail	to
here	no	not	so	hole	way	some	write

two
to

blew
_____

knot
_____

meat
_____

mail
_____

weigh
_____

sum
_____

heal
_____

know
_____

sew
_____

whole
_____

hear
_____

rode
_____

right
_____

sale
_____

tale
_____

Skills: introducing and reinforcing homonyms, visual discrimination, creativity

23

TO THE BEACH

Follow the path from the parking lot to the beach by writing the **homonym** for each word on the line below it. Use the Word Box to help you.

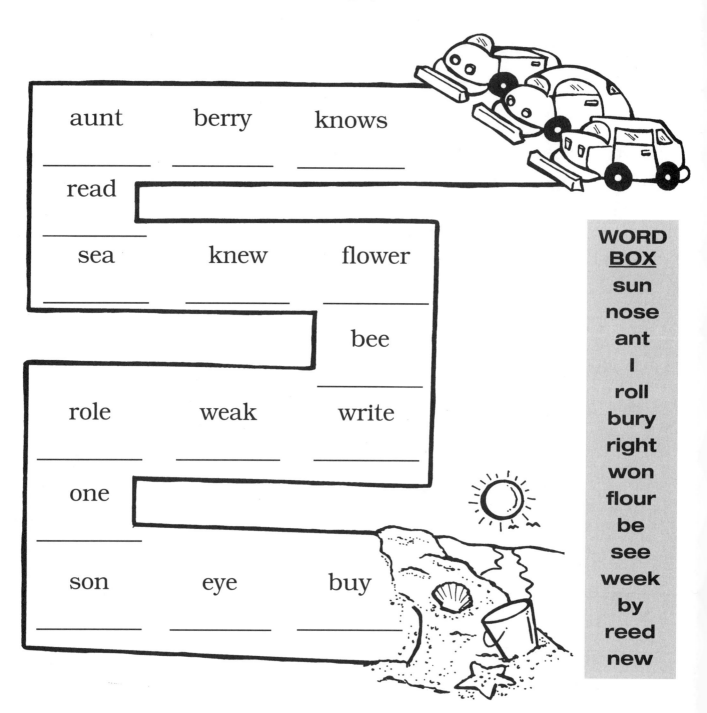

aunt   berry   knows

_____   _____   _____

read

_____

sea   knew   flower

_____   _____   _____

                              bee

                              _____

role   weak   write

_____   _____   _____

one

_____

son   eye   buy

_____   _____   _____

**WORD
BOX**
sun
nose
ant
I
roll
bury
right
won
flour
be
see
week
by
reed
new

Skills: reinforcing homonyms, visual discrimination

THE HOARSE HORSE

Circle the **homonyms** in the following sentences:

Hal the horse has had a sore throat all week. His voice has been hoarse and weak. So instead of running around the fields, he has been lounging on the grass watching the birds soar through the sky.

How many pairs of **homonyms** did you find? _____

Now read each sentence below. If the word in **bold** print makes sense in the sentence, put **OK** on the line next to it. If the **bold** word does not make sense, write a word that does on the line. The first two are done for you.

- The policeman **blue** his whistle. _blew_
- There was a **knot** in the rope. _OK_
- I like to eat **pairs**. _____
- The **night** is very cold and dark.

  _____
- Do you **know** all the letters of the alphabet? _____
- Please give me a **peace** of candy. _____
- How much do you **way**? _____
- There are **eight** people in my family.

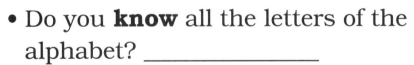

Test: Synonyms, Antonyms, and Homonyms

Fill in the word that best fits each description below. When you are done, circle each of your answers in the word search. The words in the word search can go up (↑), down (↓), or sideways (→).

- Opposite of **night**: _____
- Antonym of **beautiful**: _____
- Synonym of **center**: _____
- Opposite of **black**: _____
- Homonym of **bury**: _____
- Homonym of **knows**: _____
- Antonym of **strong**: _____
- Homonym of **whole**: _____
- Means the same as **correct**: _____
- Homonym of **won**: _____
- Means the same as **child**: _____
- Antonym of **cold**: _____

```
t  r  m  v  n  c  d  f  g  i  v  t  i  p
l  i  e  q  o  b  k  h  b  x  s  o  n  e
o  g  e  p  w  h  i  t  e  d  v  h  o  s
e  h  o  l  e  o  d  n  r  w  o  k  s  n
p  t  l  d  a  y  m  l  r  g  c  j  e  u
n  s  o  n  k  u  g  l  y  z  d  b  m  r
q  r  k  m  s  j  k  a  m  i  d  d  l  e
```

Skills: demonstrating mastery of words through testing, discrimination

When it comes to knowing Synonyms, Antonyms, and Homonyms

_____

(my name)

is

NUMBER ONE!

COMPOUND GLASSES

When two small words are put together to make one bigger word, that new word is called a **compound word**. Create **compound words** by combining the words in the eyeglasses. Write the **compound words** on the lines. Fill in the blanks where needed.

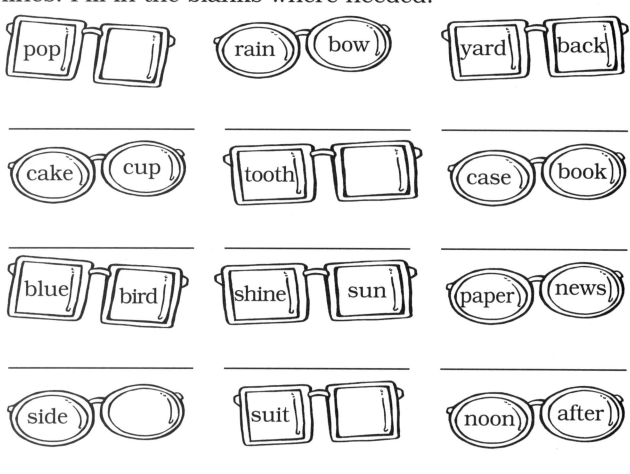

GRADE BOOSTER!

*Make as many **compound words** as you can with the words below. Write each compound on a separate piece of paper.*

bath   front   side   cow   tooth

Skills: introducing and reinforcing compound words, deduction, creativity

COMPOUNDS UPON COMPOUNDS

Sometimes one word can be combined with many different words to make a few **compound words**. Look at each group of words below. Then find the word in the Word Box that could be combined with all the words in each group to make **compound words**. Write that word on the line provided. The first one is done for you.

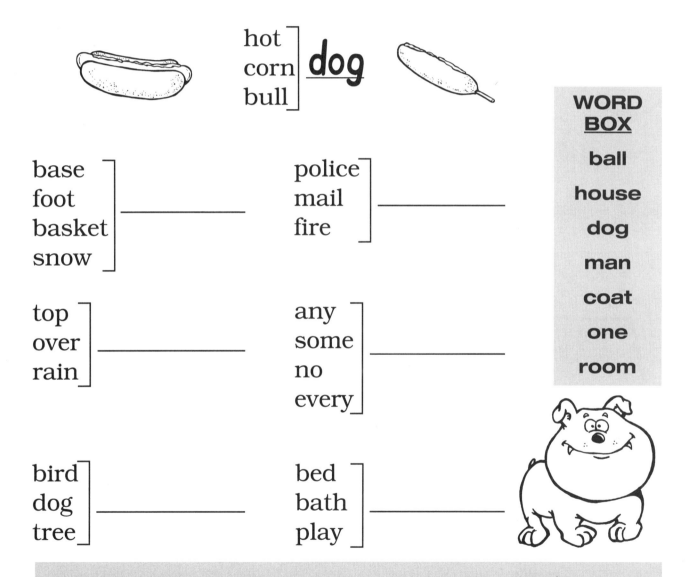

hot
corn   *dog*
bull

WORD BOX

ball

house

dog

man

coat

one

room

base
foot
basket
snow
_____

police
mail
fire
_____

top
over
rain
_____

any
some
no
every
_____

bird
dog
tree
_____

bed
bath
play
_____

TOGETHER TIME: Ask an adult to help you alphabetize each group of words on a separate piece of paper.

Skills: reinforcing compound words, deduction

THE PUP IN THE CUP

Rhyming words have the same ending sound. Look at the ending sounds in the confetti below. Then write two rhyming words for each ending on the lines provided.

ad ___

ug ___ ___

op ___ ___

ar ___

ell ___ ___

ot ___

est ___

et ___

ox ___

in ___

us ___

un ___ ___

ill ___

GRADE BOOSTER!

*Look at the words below. Then find two words that **rhyme** with each one. Write them on the lines.*

2

ham _____ _____

mitt _____ _____

Skills: introducing and reinforcing rhyming words, auditory discrimination, creativity

BOOKS, BOOKS, AND MORE BOOKS

Singular words are words that mean one. **Plural words** are words that mean more than one. You can make most nouns **plural** by adding **s** to the end of the word. For example, the plural of **book** is **books** . Now write the **plural** forms of each **singular** word below.

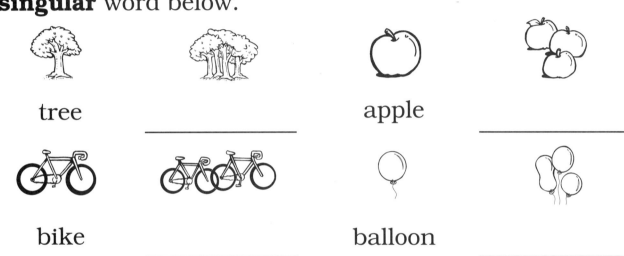

tree _____

apple _____

bike _____

balloon _____

If a noun ends with a consonant and then the letter **y,** you make it **plural** by changing the **y** to **i** and adding **es**. For example, the plural of the word **baby** is **babies** . Write the plural forms of the **singular** words below.

lady _____

candy _____

fly _____

family _____

DUAL DRESSES

When a singular noun ends in **s, ss, ch, sh, x,** or **z,** you add **es** to the end to make it plural. For example, the plural of the word **dress** is **dresses**. Write the **plural** forms of the words below.

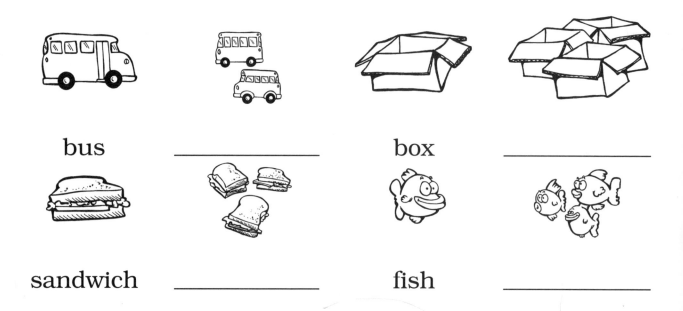

bus _____

box _____

sandwich _____

fish _____

Sometimes a word changes form when it becomes **plural**. Draw a line from each picture to the word that is its **plural**.

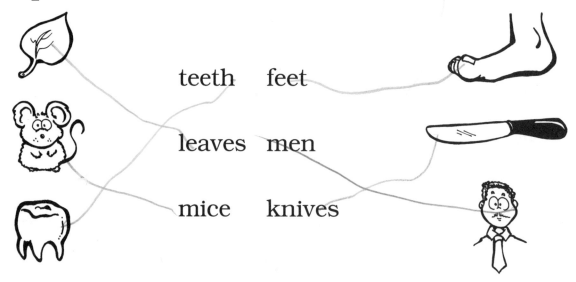

teeth   feet

leaves   men

mice   knives

BUTTERFLY CONTRACTIONS

Contractions are words that are formed when two small words are put together, but one or more letters are left out. The missing letters are replaced with an **apostrophe (')**.

Write the **contractions** formed when you combine each of the pairs of words below. The first one is done for you.

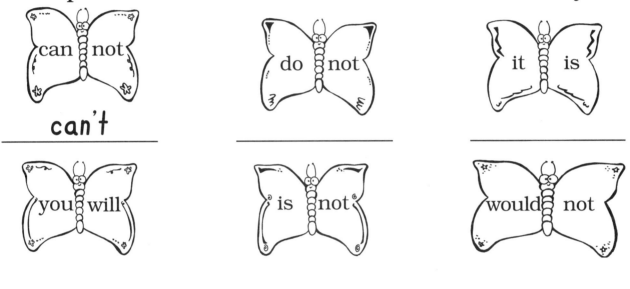

can not

can't
_____

do not

_____

it is

_____

you will

_____

is not

_____

would not

_____

Now write the two words that make up each contraction.

I'm   couldn't   she'll

_____   _____   _____

that's   hasn't   wasn't

_____   _____   _____

GRADE BOOSTER!

*On a separate piece of paper, write a sentence or question using each **contraction** above.*

Skills: introducing association of contractions with source words, creativity   **33**

LET'S USE CONTRACTIONS

Read the story below. Circle all of the contractions that you see. Then write each contraction and the two words that form the contraction on the lines below.

On Sunday morning, Jamie and her family were going to the zoo. Jamie couldn't wait. She hadn't been to the zoo before and she knew she'd love it. Her big brother Jeffrey told Jamie, "It's so much fun! You'll love the monkeys. They're so cute."

Jamie had a great time at the zoo. She didn't want to leave when the day was over. So her parents told her they'd be able to come back soon.

Contraction   Two Words

_____   _____

_____   _____

_____   _____

_____   _____

_____   _____

_____   _____

_____   _____

_____   _____

34

SILLY SYLLABLES

Baxter is blowing bubbles. The words **bubbles** and **Baxter** each have two **syllables,** or parts: **bub–bles** and **Bax–ter**. Look at the words in the bubbles below. Say each word out loud. Then count the number of parts or **syllables** you hear. Write that number on the line below each word.

flower ____

soap ____

sleep ____

popcorn ____

remember ____

spelling ____

candy ____

laugh ____

basketball ____

bear ____

rain ____

school ____

house ____

different ____

funny ____

grandmother ____

bubbles ____

TOGETHER TIME: Ask an adult to help you find a single die around your house. Roll the die. Then say a word that has the same number of syllables as the number that appeared on the die. Then have your adult friend do the same thing. Keep taking turns until you each have said one word for each number on the die.

SYL-LA-BLE SEN-SA-TION

Look at the words in the Word Box. Count the number of **syllables** in each word. Then write each word under the number that tells how many **syllables** it has.

WORD BOX					
milk	student	teacher	volleyball	bathtub	gum
grape	operator	mailman	professor	history	girl

1

2

3

_____ _____ _____

_____ _____ _____

_____ _____ _____

_____ _____ _____

GRADE BOOSTER!

*Now put each list of words above in alphabetical order on the lines below. One word has four **syllables**. Do you know which word? Write it here:* _____

1   **2**   **3**

_____ _____ _____

_____ _____ _____

_____ _____ _____

_____ _____ _____

Skills: reinforcing syllables, spelling, deduction, alphabetizing

TEST: Word Classification and Identification

Complete each of the following statements. Then write each of your answers in a blank bingo box below.

- The plural of **sandwich** is _____.

- The contraction of **cannot** is _____.

- The compound of **pop** and **corn** is _____.

- There is (are) _____ syllable(s) in the word **pipe**.

- The compound of **butter** and **fly** is _____.

- There are (is) _____ syllable(s) in the word **television**.

- The contraction of **do** and **not** is _____.

- The singular of **families** is _____.

	FREE	

TOGETHER TIME: Copy each of the answers above onto small pieces of paper and put them in a bowl or a hat. Then ask an adult to play a game of word bingo with you. Use buttons or other small round objects to cover the words as you play. As soon as you cover three words all in one row, yell BINGO!

_____

(my name)

is a

MASTER OF WORDS!

CLASSY CLASSIFICATION

Classifying means grouping words together that have similar meanings or something in common. Classify each group of words below. Draw a line matching each group to the one word in the center of the page that describes **all** the words in the group.

Ping-Pong
football
soccer
basketball
tennis

MONEY

TOYS

PLACES

COLORS

SPORTS

DRINKS

bank
gas station
school
church
library

water
lemonade
Kool-Aid
milk
root beer

book
blocks
games
cars
puzzles

Now complete each sentence with a word that tells or describes what the words in **bold** print have in common.

• **Apples** and **grapes** are _____.
• **Sally** and **Maria** are _____.
• **California** and **Texas** are _____.
• **Winter** and **summer** are _____.
• **Balls** and **wheels** are _____.

Skills: introducing and reinforcing classification, associating whole-part relationships

MORE CLASSIFYING

Let's practice more **classification**. Draw a line from each group of words to the one word in the center of the page that describes **all** the words in the group.

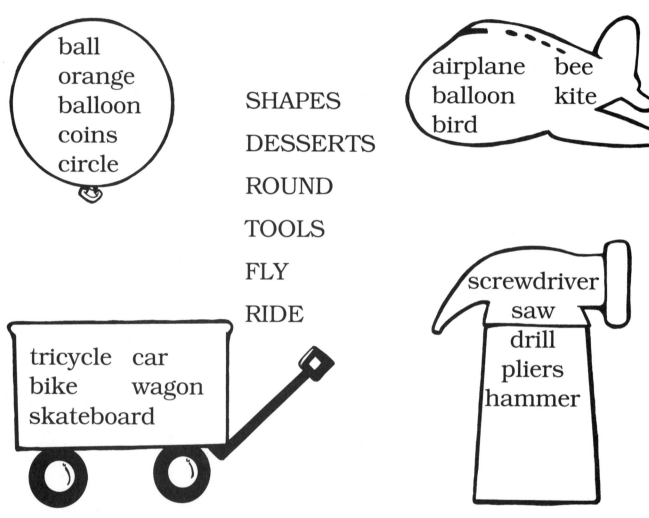

ball
orange
balloon
coins
circle

airplane   bee
balloon   kite
bird

SHAPES

DESSERTS

ROUND

TOOLS

FLY

RIDE

tricycle   car
bike   wagon
skateboard

screwdriver
saw
drill
pliers
hammer

Now complete each sentence with a word that tells or describes what the words in **bold** print have in common.

• **Ice cream** and **snow** are _____.

• **Puppies** and **kittens** are _____.

• **Plants** and **grass** are _____.

• **Dogs** and **fish** are _____.

• **Tomatoes** and **cucumbers** are _____.

Skills: reinforcing classification, associating whole-part relationships

MONTH MADNESS

Unscramble the twelve months of the year by writing them in the correct order on the lines below.

April	February	July	October	January	August
March	September	June	December	November	May

1. _____

2. _____

3. _____

4. _____

5. _____

6. _____

7. _____

8. _____

9. _____

10. _____

11. _____

12. _____

GRADE BOOSTER!

Now unscramble the seven days of the week and write them in the proper order on the lines below.

**Tuesday   Thursday   Saturday   Friday
Sunday   Wednesday   Monday**

1. _____

2. _____

3. _____

4. _____

5. _____

6. _____

7. _____

STAGELOFOLUS

Clever Charley created a character named Stagelofolus. Now show how clever you are by following the directions below to finish the picture. Use crayons to draw or color each part as indicated.

1. Put a hat on Stagelofolus. Color it brown.
2. Put three flowers to the right of Stagelofolus. Color one red, one blue, and one yellow.
3. Draw a small tree to the left of Stagelofolus. Color its leaves green.
4. Put a dog next to the tree and color it gray.
5. Draw a bird flying in the sky. Color the bird blue.
6. Put a round sun in the sky over the flowers. Color it yellow.

GRADE BOOSTER!

On a separate piece of paper, write a short story about Stagelofolus.

Skills: following directions, comprehension, recognizing details, creativity

A COUNTRY HOUSE

Create a country setting for this house by following the directions below to finish the picture. Use crayons to draw or color each part as indicated.

1. Draw green grass under and around the house.
2. Draw curtains in all the windows of the house.
3. Draw a pie sitting on the sill of the open window.
4. Put an apple tree to the right of the house. Color the leaves green, the apples red, and the tree trunk brown.
5. Draw a dirt path leading up to the front door.
6. Draw two children playing in the yard. Make one child a boy and one child a girl. The girl should be older than the boy.

GRADE BOOSTER!

On a separate piece of paper, write a short story about this country house. Who lives in the house? How long have they lived there?

CAUSE AND EFFECT

Cause: An action or act that makes something happen.
Effect: Something that happens because of an action or cause.

Look at the following example of **cause** and **effect**.

Your mother loves you. She takes good care of you.
       cause   **effect**

Now draw a line connecting each **cause** on the left side of the page to its **effect** on the right side of the page.

Skills: introducing and identifying cause and effect, reasoning, deduction

MORE EFFECTS

Draw a line connecting the pictures that go together. Then figure out which picture is the **cause** and which is the **effect**. Write **C** for **cause** or **E** for **effect** under each picture.

TOGETHER TIME: Ask an adult to help you think of three events that happened today. Why did they happen? Describe the **cause** and **effect** of each event. *Hint:* There may be more than one **cause** for each event.

FACT VS. OPINION

A **fact** is something that can be proven as true. An **opinion** is a person's belief or feeling. Read each statement below and decide if it is a **fact** (can prove it) or an **opinion** (someone's feeling). Write an **F** for **fact** or an **O** for **opinion** on the line next to each sentence.

- The ball is round. _____
- That is a cute dog. _____
- Mom works every day. _____
- Pizza tastes good. _____
- Playing at the park is fun. _____
- The car has a radio. _____
- Flowers smell good. _____
- The music is too loud. _____
- Laurie and Suzie are friends. _____

Yellowstone is the best place to camp.

I like the Grand Canyon much better.

GRADE BOOSTER!

*Change each **opinion** sentence to a **fact** sentence. Write each new sentence on a separate piece of paper.*

Skills: introducing and reinforcing fact vs. opinion, analysis, creativity

MORE FACTS AND OPINIONS

Look at the pictures below. Then write one **fact** (can prove it) sentence and one **opinion** (someone's feelings) sentence about each picture. One is done for you.

FACT: _The boy is reading the book._
OPINION: _The boy likes the book he is reading._

FACT: _____

_____

OPINION: _____

_____

FACT: _____

_____

OPINION: _____

_____

FACT: _____

_____

OPINION: _____

_____

TEST: Reasoning Skills

Fill in the crossword puzzle below. Use the words in the Word Box to help you.

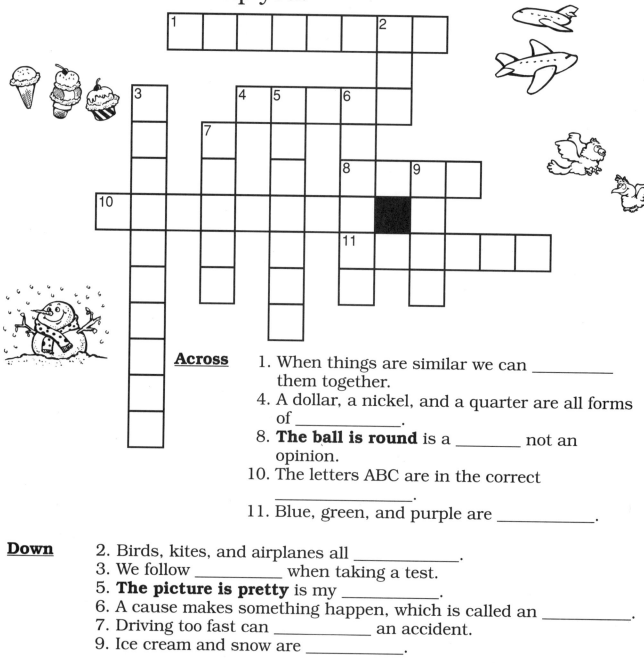

Across

1. When things are similar we can _____ them together.
4. A dollar, a nickel, and a quarter are all forms of _____.
8. **The ball is round** is a _____ not an opinion.
10. The letters ABC are in the correct _____.
11. Blue, green, and purple are _____.

Down

2. Birds, kites, and airplanes all _____.
3. We follow _____ when taking a test.
5. **The picture is pretty** is my _____.
6. A cause makes something happen, which is called an _____.
7. Driving too fast can _____ an accident.
9. Ice cream and snow are _____.

WORD BOX

directions	classify	fly	effect	fact	cold
sequence	cause	opinion	money	colors	

Skills: demonstrating mastery of reasoning skills through testing

This certifies that

_____
(my name)

is a whiz at

Reasoning Skills

MARTY GETS THE MAIN IDEA

The **main idea** is what a story is about. Help Marty figure out the **main idea** of the passages below. Write a check mark (✓) next to each main idea.

Finding the main idea is my game.

Chrissi's father is a policeman. He goes to work every day and wears a uniform. Sometimes he gives people tickets. Sometimes his job is dangerous.

____ Everyone likes policemen.

____ Chrissi's dad is a policeman.

____ Policemen help people.

There are many things that are green. Grass and leaves are green. A traffic signal is sometimes green. Many vegetables are green. Some money is green.

____ Vegetables are always green.

____ Green is a good color.

____ Many things are green.

I like to listen to music. It makes me happy. When I hear music, I want to tap my foot and dance. I like to sing along with the melody.

____ I sing to music.

____ I enjoy music.

____ I want to learn to play music.

Skills: comprehending the main idea, recognizing details

SARAH USES HER SENSES

Sarah uses all five of her senses every day. Help her figure out which part(s) of her body she uses with each sense. Draw a line matching each sense to the body part that relates to it.

sight   touch

hearing

taste   smell

Now draw a line matching each picture to the sense (or senses) that relates to it.

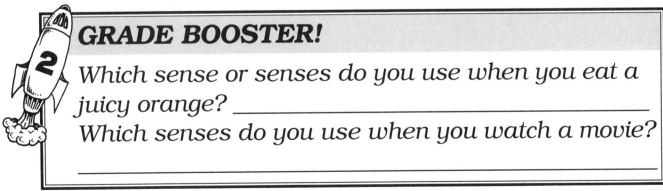

hearing

sight

taste

smell

touch

GRADE BOOSTER!

2

Which sense or senses do you use when you eat a juicy orange? _____

Which senses do you use when you watch a movie?

_____

FOOD FOR THOUGHT

Read the paragraph below. Then complete each statement that follows by underlining the phrase that makes the most sense. Use the information given as well as your own knowledge to help you make your choice. This choice is called your **conclusion**.

The chipmunk ran along the ground looking for food. He found a nut in the leaves. He stuffed it into his cheek. When his cheek was full of nuts, he hurried off to bury them in the ground near a tree. Then he went in search of more nuts. He buried those nuts, as well.

• The chipmunk was gathering nuts because (a) he was hungry; (b) he was playing a game; (c) he was storing them for the winter.

• This story takes place in (a) winter; (b) spring; (c) summer; (d) fall.

• In the winter, the chipmunk will probably (a) starve; (b) forget where he has stored his nuts; (c) have lots to eat.

URSULA USES CONTEXT CLUES

Read each sentence below. Then help Ursula fill in the blank by circling the word that makes the most sense. The other words in the sentence, called the **context,** will help you figure out which word fits best.

Dad wants to buy Tom a new _____ to ride because his old one is broken.

a) puppy   b) coat   c) bike   d) bed

Leanne wants to make a special cake for her mom's birthday. She asked her dad, "Will you _____ me?"

a) give   b) help   c) cook   d) bake

"Can I have some _____ to eat?" said Daniel, who was hungry.

a) cookies   b) apple   c) toys   d) hamburger

Cindy went to her _____ house today, so she did not play with her friends.

a) grandmother's   b) friend's   c) store   d) school

CARLOS THE CAR

Fill in the blanks below with the words that make the most sense in each paragraph. Use the the words in each Word Box to help you.

My name is _____. I am a _____. I am just a few years _____. My paint color is_____. My seats are as _____ as the grass. I hold _____ people.

WORD BOX

Carlos	old
green	white
car	two

In the morning my engine is _____ from sitting outside all _____. To start my motor, Carl puts his _____ in the car and turns it on. He steps on the _____. I start to move, but not too quickly. I'm still not quite _____. Soon I can go really _____.

WORD BOX

awake	cold
gas	night
key	fast

Skills: using context clues, drawing conclusions

GETTING THE FACTS

Read each paragraph below. Then answer the questions that follow.

Carolyn's pet is a cat. Her cat lives in her apartment with her. Every day she feeds it cat food. The cat's name is Peaches. Sometimes she plays with the cat.

- Who has a pet cat? _____
- Where does it live? _____
- What does it eat? _____
- Who plays with the cat? _____

Barbara's family has a new car. It is maroon colored. The seats are black. Five people fit in their new car. It has two seat belts in front and three seat belts in the back. They call the car the "Speedy Racer."

- What did the family get? _____
- What color is the car? _____
- How many seat belts are in

  the car? _____
- What color are the seats?

  _____

PAMELA'S PARTY

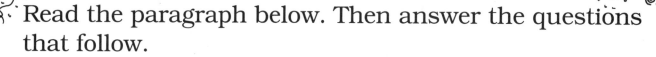

Read the paragraph below. Then answer the questions that follow.

Pamela had a birthday party on Saturday. She had eight friends come to her party at the park. Her mother brought the food and the children brought presents. They had pizza, soft drinks, and a birthday cake with seven candles.

• What kind of party did Pamela have?

_____

• Where was the party?

_____

• How many friends came to her party? _____

• What did they eat? _____

• How old is Pamela? _____

• What is the main idea of this story?_____

_____

• How do you think Pamela felt on Saturday? _____

_____

TOGETHER TIME: Ask an adult to help you plan your own pretend birthday party. Who will come to your party? What food will you serve? What games will you play?

Skills: comprehension, recognizing details, deduction, creativity

THE SMITH FAMILY PICNIC

Read the paragraph below. Then answer the questions that follow.

On Sunday afternoon our whole family is going to the beach to have a picnic. The beach is far from our house, so we have to go there in our car. We need to bring food and some toys to the picnic. There are seven people in my family. We also have several pets—two dogs, a cat, and a turtle. We will stay at the beach all day long.

- What kind of food do you think the family will bring to the picnic? _____
- Which toys will they bring with them? _____
  _____
- Which pets will the family take with them on their picnic? _____
- How long will they stay at the beach? _____
- How do you think the family will feel after they return home from the beach? _____

GRADE BOOSTER!

What are your favorite kinds of foods to eat on a picnic at the beach? _____
What are your favorite things to do at the beach?
_____

Test: Comprehension Skills

Read the story below and then answer the questions that follow.

THE CAMPING TRIP

Ken, Dave, and Tom were going on a camping trip to Sequoia National Park with their dad. They packed their car with their camping equipment and food before they went to bed. Early in the morning they left on their trip. They drove for a long time and finally got to the campground. Ken and Dave set up the tent. Tom unrolled all the sleeping bags inside the tent. Their dad went to register at the campsite and found out about all the activities and campfire programs.

• When did they leave to go camping? _____

• Who went to the ranger station to register? _____

• Who set up the tent? _____

• What did Tom do? _____

• Where did they go to camp? _____

• After camp is set up, what do you think they will do?

_____

• Why do you think they went camping? _____

_____

Skills: demonstrating mastery of comprehension skills through testing

ANSWERS

Page 6

B S W K M
G C Z P Q
L T D N W
V X R F H

GB: J and Y are not pictured. Rest of answer will vary.

Page 7

long ā words: rain, baby, rake, tail
long ē words: bee, feet, pea, seal
long ī words: slide, fire, kite, child

Page 8

long ō words: soap, toe, bone, note
long ū words: music, fruit, cute, juice
y as in long ē: happy, baby, puppy, crazy, funny, sleepy, lucky, silly
y as in long ī: my, sky, by, cry, dry, try

Page 9

short ă words: cat, pan, man
short ĕ words: nest, bed, tent
short ĭ words: pin, mitten, swim
Eel, kite, and *airplane* all have long vowel sounds.

Page 10

short ŏ words: box, doll, octopus
short ŭ words: sun, nut, skunk
Boot and toe have long vowel sounds.
GB: Answers will vary.

Page 11

red long vowel words: cane, key, slide, cube, rain, baby, smoke, puppy
blue short vowel words: mop, puppy, cat, jet, skunk
Puppy has both a short and a long vowel sound.

Page 12

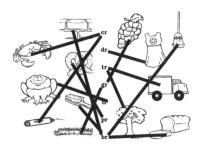

GB: br has the most words: 4
pr, fr, and **dr** have the least words: 1 each

Page 13

Clarice the Clown needs glasses to see clearly through the clouds.
blanket, blocks, clock, flag, flower, glasses, plane, sleep, slide
GB: Answers will vary.

Page 14

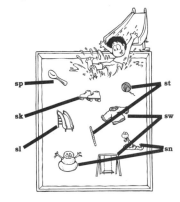

Page 15

Chucky the Chipmunk chuckled and shrieked when he got his shoe caught in the wheel.
wh: whiskers
th: throat, thumb
ch: cheese, cherry
sh: shell, shoe
GB: Answers will vary.

Page 16

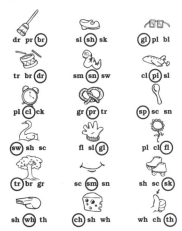

Answers

Page 18

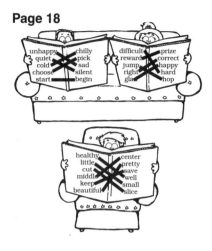

Page 19

little, car, finish, rush, shout, quick
TT: Answers will vary but may include: exam: test; large: big or huge; maybe: possibly; choose: pick; scared: frightened; friend: companion; fall: autumn; high: tall

Page 20

easy: hard; fast: slow; short: tall; loud: quiet; hot: cold; play: work; night: day; right: wrong; in: out; empty: full

Page 21

Answers will vary but may include: closes, clean, far, on, small

Page 22

GB: There are 7 sets of synonyms and 8 sets of antonyms. One set of words is homonyms.

Page 23

two: to; blew: blue; knot: not; meat: meet; mail: male; weigh: way; sum: some; heal: heel; know: no; sew: so; whole: hole; hear: here; rode: road; right: write; sale: sail; tale: tail

Page 24

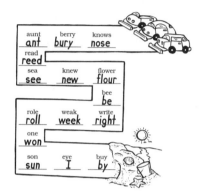

Page 25

Hal the (horse) has had a (sore) throat all (week) His voice has been (hoarse) and (weak) So instead of running around the fields, he has been lounging on the grass watching the birds (soar) through the sky.

3 pairs of homonyms
pears, OK, OK, piece, weigh, OK

Page 26

day, ugly, middle, white, berry, nose, weak, hole, right, one, kid, hot

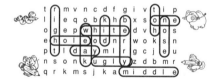

Page 28

popcorn, rainbow, backyard, cupcake, toothbrush, bookcase, bluebird, sunshine, newspaper, sidewalk, suitcase, afternoon
GB: Answers will vary.

Page 29

TT: *Parent:* Make sure answer reflects child's knowledge of how to alphabetize correctly.

Page 30

Answers will vary.
GB: Answers will vary but may include: ham: lamb, dam, ram; mitt: hit, bit, kit

Page 31

trees, apples, bikes, balloons ladies, candies, flies, families

Page 32

buses, boxes, sandwiches, fishes

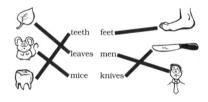

Page 33

don't, it's, you'll, isn't, wouldn't
I am, could not, she will, that is, has not, was not
GB: Answers will vary.

Page 34

On Sunday morning, Jamie and her family were going to the zoo. Jamie (couldn't) wait. She (hadn't) been to the zoo before and she knew (she'd) love it. Her big brother Jeffrey told Jamie, "(It's) so much fun! (You'll) love the monkeys. (They're) so cute."

Jamie had a great time at the zoo. She (didn't) want to leave when the day was over. So her parents told her (they'd) be able to come back soon.

couldn't	could not
hadn't	had not
she'd	she would
It's	It is
You'll	You will
They're	They are
didn't	did not
they'd	they would

Page 35

One-syllable words: sleep, soap, laugh, rain, school, house, bear
Two-syllable words: flower, spelling, popcorn, candy, bubbles, funny
Three-syllable words: different, remember, basketball, grandmother
TT: Answers will vary.

Page 36

1: girl, grape, gum, milk
2: bathtub, mailman, student, teacher
3: history, professor, volleyball
GB: See order above. Operator has four syllables.

Page 37

sandwiches, can't, popcorn, one, butterfly, four, don't, family
TT: Answers will vary.

Page 39

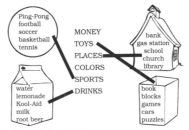

fruits, girls, states, seasons, round

Page 40

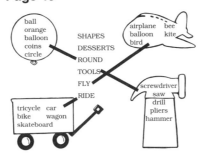

cold, pets or animals, green, pets or animals, vegetables

Page 41

January, February, March, April, May, June, July, August, September, October, November, December
GB: Monday, Tuesday, Wednesday, Thursday, Friday, Saturday, Sunday

Page 42

Parent: Make sure child's additions reflect his or her understanding of the text.

Page 43

Parent: Make sure child's additions reflect his or her understanding of the text.

Page 44

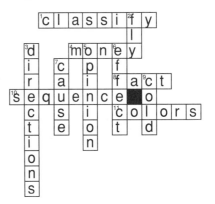

Page 45

TT: Answers will vary.

Page 46

- The ball is round. __F__
- That is a cute dog. __O__
- Mom works every day. __F__
- Pizza tastes good. __O__
- Playing at the park is fun. __O__
- The car has a radio. __F__
- Flowers smell good. __O__
- The music is too loud. __O__
- Laurie and Suzie are friends. __F__

GB: Answers will vary.

Page 47

Parent: Make sure child's sentences reflect his or her understanding of the text.

Page 48

classify, line, money, dir, pai, fact, sequence, colors, caption, sections, off, fod, cot

63

Answers

Page 50
Chrissi's dad is a policeman.
Many things are green.
I enjoy music.

Page 51

GB: When you eat an orange, you use your sense of taste, smell, and sight.
When you watch a movie, you use your sense of sight and hearing.

Page 52
c: he was storing them for the winter.
d: fall.
c: have lots to eat.

Page 53
c: bike
b: help
a: cookies
a: grandmother's

Page 54
My name is *Carlos*. I am a *car*. I am just a few years *old*. My paint color is *white*. My seats are as *green* as the grass. I hold *two* people.

In the morning my engine is *cold* from sitting outside all *night*. To start my motor, Carl puts his *key* in the car and turns it on. He steps on the *gas*. I start to move, but not too quickly. I'm still not quite *awake*. Soon I can go really *fast*.

Page 55
Carolyn has a pet cat.
It lives in her apartment.
It eats cat food.
Carolyn plays with the cat.

The family got a new car.
The car is maroon.
There are five seat belts.
The seats are black.

Page 56
Pamela had a birthday party.
The party was at the park.
Eight friends came to the party.
They ate pizza and birthday cake.
Pamela is seven years old.
Rest of answers will vary.
TT: Answers will vary.

Page 57
Answers will vary.
Parent: Answers should reflect child's understanding of the paragraph.
GB: Answers will vary.

Page 58
They left to go camping early in the morning.
Their dad went to the ranger station to register.
Ken and Dave set up the tent.
Tom unrolled the sleeping bags inside the tent.
They went to Sequoia National Park.
Rest of answers will vary.